FIRST SKYLARK CHOOSE YOUR OWN ADVENTURE® • 52

"I DON'T LIKE CHOOSE YOUR OWN ADVENTURE® BOOKS, I *LOVE* THEM!" says Jessica Gordon, age ten. And now kids between the ages of five and nine can choose their own adventures too. Here's what kids have to say about the Skylark Choose Your Own Adventure® books.

"These are my favorite books because you can pick whatever choice you want—and the story is all about you."
—**Kathy Alson,** *age 8*

"I love finding out how my story will end."
—**Joss Williams,** *age 9*

"I like all the illustrations!"
—**Savitri Brightfield,** *age 7*

"A six-year-old friend and I have lots of fun making the decisions together."
—**Peggy Marcus** *(adult)*

Bantam Skylark Books in the Choose Your Own Adventure® series
Ask your bookseller for the books you have missed

#2 THE HAUNTED HOUSE
#6 THE GREEN SLIME
#18 SUMMER CAMP
#37 HAUNTED HALLOWEEN PARTY
#40 THE GREAT EASTER BUNNY ADVENTURE
#46 A DAY WITH THE DINOSAURS
#47 SPOOKY THANKSGIVING
#48 YOU ARE INVISIBLE
#49 RACE OF THE YEAR
#50 STRANDED!
#51 YOU CAN MAKE A DIFFERENCE:
    THE STORY OF MARTIN LUTHER KING, JR.
#52 THE ENCHANTED ATTIC

THE ENCHANTED ATTIC

ADELE READ

ILLUSTRATED BY JUDITH MITCHELL

An R.A. Montgomery Book

A BANTAM SKYLARK BOOK®
NEW YORK · TORONTO · LONDON · SYDNEY · AUCKLAND

RL 2, 005–008

THE ENCHANTED ATTIC

A Bantam First Skylark Book / July 1992

CHOOSE YOUR OWN ADVENTURE® is a registered trademark of Bantam Books, a division of Bantam Doubleday Dell Publishing Group, Inc. Registered in U.S. Patent and Trademark Office and elsewhere.

Original conception of Edward Packard

Skylark Books is a registered trademark of Bantam Books, a division of Bantam Doubleday Dell Publishing Group, Inc. Registered in U.S. Patent and Trademark Office and elsewhere.

Cover art by Bill Schmidt
Interior illustrations by Judith Mitchell

ISBN 0-553-15636-5

Published simultaneously in the United States and Canada

Bantam Books are published by Bantam Books, a division of Bantam Doubleday Dell Publishing Group, Inc. Its trademark, consisting of the words "Bantam Books" and the portrayal of a rooster, is Registered in U.S. Patent and Trademark Office and in other countries. Marca Registrada. Bantam Books, 666 Fifth Avenue, New York, New York 10103.

PRINTED IN THE UNITED STATES OF AMERICA

CWO   0 9 8 7 6 5 4 3 2

THE
ENCHANTED
ATTIC

Aunt Mae's Dress
Satin Material

Draper from Elm St

green dishes

kitchen utensils

Mother's Teaset

READ THIS FIRST!!!

Most books are about other people.

This book is about you, and the adventures you have when you explore your grandparents' attic.

Do not read this book from the first page to the last. Instead, start on page one and read until you come to your first choice. When you decide what you want to do, turn to the page shown, and see what happens next.

When you come to the end of a story, go back and try another choice. Every choice leads to a new adventure.

Are you ready to discover the mysteries of an ancient leather trunk? Then turn to page one—and good luck!

Summer vacation is finally here!

But this year, the only ones in your family who get to go on vacation are your parents. They're going on an archaeological dig in South America. *They* get to study old bones and uncover buried clues to our ancient past, while *you're* stuck at your grandparents' house.

Gramma and Gramps are okay, but they're stuffy and hard to talk to. To top things off, it's been raining for three days, and you're bored stiff. You've read a pile of books and magazines, watched hours of television, and lost twenty-seven games of checkers to Gramma.

You're staring glumly out the window when Gramps says, "Why don't you explore the attic? You never know what you might find up there."

You can't think of anything better to do, so you climb the stairs to the second floor, to the third floor, and then even more stairs to the attic—and open the door.

Turn to page 15.

2   "An archaeologist," you tell your mother.
"And a famous one too."

"Wow!"

"Look," you say, "meeting you has really
been great. But I don't know how I got here,
and I don't belong here. I have to return to
my own time—somehow."

"I bet my parents could help you," your
mother says. "They're really smart. They can
do anything."

"I don't know," you say. Gramma and
Gramps have always seemed pretty dull to
you. "I'm sure they won't believe us."

"I bet they would. But there *is* something
else. We could try a magic spell. I know lots
of them."

"Hmmmm," you say.

"It's up to you," Jill goes on. "But if we try
a spell, we'll have to wait until the party's
over. I've got to get back to my party now."

---

*If you decide to ask your grandparents for
help, turn to page 48.*

*If you want to try one of your mom's magic
spells, turn to page 51.*

"How do I go back?" you ask. "I'll do anything."

"I'm glad to hear that," the wizard says. "I know of only one way. But it's dangerous and tricky."

"What is it?" you ask.

"You must steal the Changing Ring from the troll in the Outer Region. Then you must use the ring only at the fullest moment of a full moon."

This does sound tough. But if it's the only way to go home, then you'll have to do it.

"Where is the Outer Region?" you ask.

The wizard hands you a map. "This is where the troll lives," he says, pointing. "That X is a tall tree. The troll lives at the very top. You can either climb to the top or fly up. I recommend climbing. But if you must fly, repeat this chant: 'Elmadon and Elmadop, take me to the very top.'"

The wizard gives you some more directions. Then he fades away.

Turn to page 36.

Suddenly you feel as if you are rising out **5** of the chair. The attic disappears! And you're spinning through space.

You can hear voices singing. "Happy birthday, dear Ji-ill. Happy birthday to you!"

Plop! You land on a green lawn. In front of you is your grandparents' house. In back of you are a bunch of kids sitting around a table. They're having a party.

"Hey, Jill Carson!" yells a voice. "How does it feel to turn ten?"

Jill Carson is your mom's name . . . or at least it was before she married your dad. You can't believe it. You're at your mother's tenth birthday party! You've traveled back in time more than twenty years!

Just then, your mother sees you sitting in the grass. "Hey, you!" she cries, running across the lawn. "Who are you?"

How am I ever going to explain *this?* you wonder.

If you tell your mother the truth,
turn to page 24.

If you tell your mother you're a new kid in the neighborhood, turn to page 27.

6 You turn to find yourself face-to-face with an elf—one who seems very tall. You do seem to have shrunk!

Where am I? you wonder. You're not in the attic any longer, or in the trunk. You seem to be in the woods.

"Hello," you say. "Excuse me, but where am I?"

"In Elmadon," the elf says. "You've gone over . . . Hey! Oh, hey! Syrus!" he calls suddenly.

The elf is calling to a horse who's trotting down the road. The horse is very small, no taller than your waist.

"Where are you going?" the elf asks.

"I'm on my way to see the Lord of the Wishes," the horse replies.

"We'll come with you," the elf says. He pulls at your shirt sleeve.

Turn to page 20.

8   You keep digging through the trunk until—

WHOOSH!

You feel your body lift from the floor. Suddenly you are sucked inside the trunk, headfirst. You feel as if you are swimming through the clothes. The clothes seem very big to you and you feel very small. Have I shrunk? you wonder. You can't see a thing.

Turn to page 14.

You reach up and grab the ring, then **9** shinny down the tree.

"Hey!" the troll shouts. "Give me back my ring!" But he doesn't leave his safe nest to come after you.

You slip and slide to the ground.

"I have the ring!" you cry triumphantly.

All you have to do now is wait for the fullest moment of a full moon, put the Changing Ring on your left pinkie, and turn it twice, just like the wizard instructed.

Turn to page 54.

10   You take a rest and then start climbing again. There must be some reason the wizard suggested you climb rather than fly.

It takes hours, but finally you reach the top of the tree. You cling to a branch below the troll's nest.

Now what? you think.

Before you can decide what to do, you hear a rustling sound in the nest. A wrinkled, brown face peers over the edge.

It's the troll!

"Thought you'd never get here," he croaks. "I suppose you want the ring."

"Well . . . yes!" you say, surprised.

The troll slips a gold ring off his finger. "Here it is. You can have it—but only if you'll grant *me* a wish."

Turn to page 21.

"I'll stay here," you say. You wave good-bye to the horse and the elf. Then you turn around and set off through the woods.

After a while the trees thin out. Soon you come to a road. At the side of the road a robin the size of a cat catches a worm even larger than itself.

You shake your head. The sizes seem to be all wrong here in Elmadon!

Suddenly you see something moving toward you. It's a man—but he's only three inches tall. He tells you he's a giant, though.

"A giant?" you exclaim.

"Well, I was . . . before I went over."

The little man smiles, then walks on.

Just then, a shape appears before you. It comes from out of thin air.

You scream and jump back.

The shape turns into an old man with a snowy-white beard and a cone-shaped hat.

"Don't be afraid," he says. "I'm a wizard. I can help you."

Turn to page 3.

14   A loud cracking noise startles you. You cover your ears.

After a few moments, you have stopped moving. You can't feel the clothes around you anymore. You uncover your ears. The loud cracking noise is gone.

"Welcome," says a little voice, startling you.

Very slowly, you turn around.

Turn to page 6.

The attic is pitch-dark. You feel around for **15** a light switch.

Click!

You walk into the musty, dusty attic and look around. Cartons are stacked everywhere. Most of them are labeled *china, Mother's tea set,* and dull things like that. But pushed far back in the corner is a beat-up old leather trunk. Now *that* could be interesting!

Turn to page 31.

16   You've got nothing but time. You find an armchair and sink into it. Then you open the photo album. On the first page is written *Jill—10th year.* Hmmmm. Jill is your mother's name. You turn the page.

You jump. The person grinning at the camera in the picture is you! No, you realize, it's someone with short hair who looks just like you. The picture is labeled *Jill.* This must be a picture of your mother.

In the next picture your mother is riding a pony. Running along beside her are a man and a woman. The woman is laughing; the man is making a face at the camera. They look a little like Gramma and Gramps. But they're so young. And you can't imagine Gramps sticking his tongue out at anyone.

You turn back to the first picture of your mother. That's funny. She isn't smiling anymore. In fact, her mouth is open—and it's *moving.*

From far, far away you hear a girl's voice call your name.

Turn to page 5.

Officer Cranston makes you spend the night in the hospital. The doctors and nurses can't find anything wrong with your head, but they still don't believe your story.

The next day Cranston visits you in the hospital.

"You just stay here and rest," he says. "Don't worry. We'll find your parents." He pats you on the head and leaves.

Great, you think. Cranston's got a long search ahead of him—it'll be years before your parents are your parents, and by then you'll be as old as they are!

Oh, well. You'll have a chance no kid has ever had. You'll get to watch your mother grow up!

The End

20   Who is the Lord of the Wishes? you wonder. Could he help me return to the attic? You're not sure. But you don't like the way the elf just volunteers you to go along. Besides, you don't know where the Lord of the Wishes is. He could be miles away, and then you may never find your way back home.

If you decide to visit the Lord of the Wishes, turn to page 41.

If you'd rather stay where you are and not go off with the elf, turn to page 13.

Grant him a wish? You're not able to do that! But maybe if you *pretend* to be able to grant his wish, he'll believe you—and turn over the ring. Your other option is just to grab the ring from the troll and run away.

If you say that you'll grant him his wish, turn to page 38.

If you reach up and grab the ring from the troll, turn to page 9.

22   The attic disappears. You feel yourself moving through darkness.

"Help!" you cry, as you close your eyes. When you come to a stop, you open them.

You're still in the attic, but you're sitting in the armchair again. Jill and her parents are gone. And in your lap is the old, faded album.

"I'm back," you say aloud. "I think."

You rush out of the attic and down three flights of stairs. Gramma and Gramps are in the kitchen playing checkers. They look as old as ever. You are back!

Gramps glances up as you come in. "Find anything?" he asks.

"Well . . ." you begin.

"Say," Gramps interrupts. "Did I ever tell you about the day I took a trip to the future?"

"The future?" you repeat. "You mean time traveling?"

"Exactly," says Gramps. He gives you a big smile.

Suddenly you and your grandfather have a lot to talk about!

The End

24   You tell your mother the truth. Her *eyes* are as wide as saucers.

"You're *who*?" she exclaims.

"I'm . . . well, see, you are my mother," you say. "I mean, not now. But you will be."

"That's ridiculous!" Jill cries. "I'm going to tell my parents!"

Across the yard you see a much younger Gramma and Gramps. They're serving cake and ice cream.

"Don't tell them!" you say. You know they'd never believe it. "Look, I really am your kid. I know all about you. I know how you got that scar on your chin. You fell off your tricycle. And," you go on, "I can prove I'm from the future. Look at this."

You pull a solar calculator out of your pocket. "See? It lights up instantly in the sun. And look how small it is."

"Gosh," says Jill. "I guess you really are from the future. So then I'm really your *mother*?"

"Yup," you say proudly.

"What am I going to be when I grow up?" Jill asks.

Turn to page 2.

26   You jump a mile in the air.

"What was that?" you cry. "I'm getting out of here!"

Rondill laughs. "Don't be silly," he says. "That always happens when a wish is granted. That's the magic at work."

You raise your eyebrows. You've never heard of such a thing. This is starting to seem a little fishy. Besides, if the Lord of the Wishes is so powerful and wonderful, then why does he live in such an awful-looking shack?

Rondill pushes you forward toward the hut. "Go ahead," he says. "Go and ask for your wish."

Rondill's being bossy again. But he doesn't seem to be scared, so why should you be?

Turn to page 47.

"I just moved here," you tell your mother. "I'm exploring the neighborhood."

"Why don't you stay for some cake and ice cream?" your mother asks.

You wonder if you should. What if Gramma and Gramps recognize you? But then you remember, this is twenty years ago. You haven't even been born yet!

You have a great time at the party. Your mother is lots of fun. So are Gramma and Gramps. They even ask you to stay for dinner.

Go on to the next page.

28   That night you sit around the table with your mother, your grandparents, and your Uncle Chris. It's difficult for you to think of him as your uncle when he's only five years old now.

Jill and Chris start teasing each other.

"You're goofy!" Chris says.
"You're a dope," Jill replies.
"Baby!"
"Four eyes!"

Turn to page 45.

You make your way over to the trunk. You **31** can see that it's locked with a rusty clasp. Maybe Gramps has the key. As you reach out to touch the lock, it falls to the floor!

The lid of the trunk lifts easily. Inside is a pile of old-fashioned clothes. Lying on top of them is a cracked, faded photo album. You shove the dusty old album aside and dig farther down in the trunk.

Suddenly an eerie feeling washes over you. Your ears begin to ring. The attic seems to sway. Everything goes black, then returns to normal.

You step back. You're not sure what happened, but your eye is drawn to the photo album. You wonder whether you should ignore the eerie feeling and keep looking through the trunk, or if you should pick up the photo album and see what's inside.

If you decide to keep looking through the trunk, turn to page 8.

If you decide to look through the photo album, turn to page 16.

32   The lightning changes the night to day.
"Where *are* we?" Jill asks. "This isn't my
house . . . or my neighborhood. And who
are all these funny people?"

The women you see walking down the old

street wear long dresses and ruffly caps. The **33**
men wear knickers and hats with three cor-
ners.

Go on to the next page.

34 "You know," you say, "the men look like George Washington. And I don't see any telephone wires or electric lights. I have a feeling we've . . ."

". . . gone back in time!" your mother says, finishing your sentence. "And *I* wasn't supposed to go with you in the first place. I guess we should have used the right magic charms."

Oh, brother! Now you're stuck hundreds of years in the past—with your ten-year-old mother! You only hope she can work a spell to return both of you to your proper times. Meanwhile, you can be a sort of archaeologist yourself—only now you get to study the past in person!

The End

At first, all you can see is smoke. But when **35** it clears, you find yourself back in your grandparents' attic.

You don't waste a second. You quickly run down the stairs.

Gramma and Gramps are in the kitchen.

"You'll never guess what just happened to me!" you cry.

"What?" your grandparents ask.

You tell them everything—about the trunk, and Rondill, and Syrus, and the Lord of the Wishes.

Turn to page 52.

36   You follow the map and the wizard's directions carefully.

You walk for days. You aren't sure, but you think two weeks go by before you reach the troll's tree in the Outer Region.

You stand at the bottom of the tree and look up. It is the tallest tree you've ever seen.

You are dead tired, but you remember that the wizard recommended climbing up—so you begin.

You have to stop often to rest. After two hours you think you'll never make it to the top. Should I fly up? you wonder—even though the wizard warned me against it?

If you decide to recite the chant and fly to the top of the tree, turn to page 44.

If you think you should continue to climb up no matter how tired you are, turn to page 10.

38   You take a chance. "All right," you say, "what is your wish?"

"I want a million dollars," the troll replies.

You should have known! But all you say is, "Let me see what I can do."

You shinny partway down the tree. Then you sit on a branch and think. At last you have a plan. You climb back up to the nest.

"I've got your money," you tell the troll proudly. "But it's too heavy to carry up. You'll have to come down and get it yourself."

Once he's on the ground, you're sure you can wrestle the ring away from the troll.

But before the troll can say a word, a gigantic hawk swoops down out of the sky. It's the size of an airplane, and it clutches you in its talons and flies away.

Helplessly you realize you will make a fine dinner for him and his family.

The End

40   You find your way to the police station and step inside.

"Hello," you say to an officer sitting at a big desk.

"Hello there," he replies. "I'm Officer Cranston. How can I help you?"

You tell Officer Cranston your story as carefully as you can.

"Well, well, well," he says when you're finished. He walks around to the front of the desk and feels the top of your head. "Feeling all right?" he asks.

"Sure," you reply.

"No, no, I think you must have bumped your head. Ferguson!" he calls. "Come over here."

Officer Ferguson gets you some water and finds you a chair to sit in.

Cranston calls several more officers together. "We've got a lost kid here, suffering from a bump on the head. Seems a little confused. We'd better start looking for the parents."

Oh, no. This isn't going right at all.

Turn to page 19.

Maybe the Lord of the Wishes can help you find your way back home. The elf tells you his name is Rondill. You, Syrus the horse, and Rondill walk briskly through the woods.

"Why are you going to see the Lord of the Wishes?" Rondill asks Syrus.

"I want to be able to fly," the horse replies. "How about you?"

"I don't know," says Rondill. "But I'll think of something."

"Will the Lord of the Wishes grant *any* wish?" you ask.

"Any wish," replies Syrus. "He's very powerful and very generous."

"He's the wisest man we know," adds Rondill.

Maybe the Lord of the Wishes will be able to help you after all!

You walk and walk, past many trees and over many hills.

"Well, here we are," Rondill says suddenly.

Go on to the next page.

You look around, only to see a beat-up old shack.

"Where are we?" you ask.

"Why, we're at the home of the Lord of the Wishes," Syrus replies. "Where else?"

At that moment—*KA-BOOM!*—you hear **43** a loud explosion. Smoke pours out of the windows of the shack.

Turn to page 26.

44   You perch on a strong branch.

"Elmadon and Elmadop," you chant, "take me to the very top."

You leap off, flapping your arms, and . . . plunge to the ground.

The chant may work for wizards, but it doesn't work for humans.

The End

You're surprised to find out that your mom **45**
used to be a tease.

Suddenly Jill turns to you. "And *you're* a
freckle face!"

"Hey!" you cry, "I *like* my freckles. So
don't tease *me* . . . carrot top!"

"All right," says Gramps, getting to his
feet. "You kids have seen enough of each
other for one day. Jill, I think it's time for your
guest to go on home."

You can't believe it. Your own family is
turning you out.

You say good-bye to Jill and Chris, then
walk slowly down the street. At least it's still
light outside.

But it won't be light for long. Then what
are you going to do? And how are you going
to get back home and return to your own
time?

Well, you think, your parents always
taught you to go to the police if you were
ever in trouble. And you sure are in trouble
now.

Turn to page 40.

The smoke clears.

"Go on, you go first," Rondill says.

With shaky legs you walk to the hut and step inside.

The hut is very dim. At first you can make out only dark shapes. Finally you see a round table in the center of the room. An old man wearing long robes is seated there. He looks up at you, and you gasp—

The Lord of the Wishes is Gramps!

Well, he *looks* like Gramps. But is he really? You can't tell.

The Lord of the Wishes doesn't seem to recognize you. All he says is, "Come, sit down. Tell me your wish."

You look into the old man's wise brown eyes.

"I want to go home," you say simply. "The elf says I've 'gone over.'"

"So you want to go back, then?" the Lord of the Wishes replies. "Easiest thing in the world."

He snaps his fingers.

BANG!

Turn to page 35.

48   You decide to ask your grandparents for help. Jill runs to them excitedly. She pulls you along behind her.

"Mom? Dad?" she says. "Guess who this is." She tells Gramma and Gramps what you told her. She even makes you show them the calculator.

Your grandparents look thoughtful. They exchange a secret smile. "Wouldn't be the first time something like this happened," Gramps says. "I think I know just how to get you back where you belong."

When Jill's party is over, Gramps says, "Everybody up to the attic."

The four of you climb the stairs to the attic.

Gramps hands you a photo album. It looks a lot like the one you found in the trunk— only much newer. But when you open it, you gasp. The very first picture is one of you! But how can that be?

Before you can ask any questions or say good-bye, the attic starts to spin.

Turn to page 22.

Jill tells her parents that you're new in the **51** neighborhood. Gramma invites you to stay for the rest of the party and to come inside the house afterward.

Later that night, Jill takes you to her room. "We have a lot to do," she says, opening a book called *Witches' Spells.* "We have to find the eye of a bat, the tail of a rat, and the paw of a cat."

Of course you can't find them. But you settle for the eye of a teddy bear, a piece of string, and a whisker from Jill's cat.

Just before midnight you sneak outside.

"Good, there's a full moon," Jill says.

It all seems so strange to you—Jill is your mom, and she's casting spells under a full moon!

Jill holds the eye, the string, and the whisker in one hand. Then she grabs you with the other.

"Magic powers, do my bidding!" she cries.

Flash! A bolt of lightning streaks across the sky.

Turn to page 32.

52 "The funny thing is," you say, as you finish your story, "the Lord of the Wishes looked just like you, Gramps."

"Well," he replies, "I'm sure there are all sorts of things we don't know much about. There may be places in our world that lead to other worlds. I expect that there are many times when we go back and forth without even realizing it."

Gramps winks at you, hitting your shoulder playfully. "Glad I could help you get home," he says a little mysteriously.

As much as you want to find out what really happened, you decide to stay clear of the attic—at least for the time being.

The End

54 Two nights later you have your chance. You stand in a clearing, clutching the ring. When you don't think the moon could grow any more full, you put the ring on your finger and turn it twice.

The clearing starts to fade away.

You shake your head and look around. You're back in the attic. But the trunk is towering over your head! And the troll's ring is around your waist!

Oh, no! The spell went wrong. You're back in your own world—but you're only three inches tall!

The End

ABOUT THE AUTHOR

Adele Read writes children's books full-time and lives in New York City.

ABOUT THE ILLUSTRATOR

Judith Mitchell was born and raised in New York City. She earned a Bachelor of Fine Arts degree from Chatham College and has also studied art at the Columbia University School of Arts and at the School of Visual Arts in New York City. Ms. Mitchell is the illustrator of *You Are a Monster, Captive!*, *The Search for Aladdin's Lamp*, and *Superbike* in the Choose Your Own Adventure series. When she isn't working, she enjoys music, animals, cooking, collecting antiques, and traveling. Judith Mitchell lives in New York City.